IN MY NEW YELLOW SHIRT

EILEEN SPINELLI

ILLUSTRATED BY HIDEKO TAKAHASHI

HENRY HOLT AND COMPANY

NEW YORK

Henry Holt and Company, LLC
Publishers since 1866
115 West 18th Street
New York, New York 10011
www.henryholt.com

Henry Holt is a registered trademark of Henry Holt and Company, LLC

Library of Congress Cataloging-in-Publication Data
Spinelli, Eileen.
In my new yellow shirt / Eileen Spinelli; illustrated by Hideko Takahashi.
Summary: A boy wears his new yellow shirt and is transformed in his imagination
into a duck, a lion, a daffodil, a trumpet, and other things.
[1. Imagination—Fiction. 2. Clothing and dress—Fiction. 3. Yellow—Fiction.]
I. Takahashi, Hideko, ill. II. Title.
PZ7.S7566In 2001 [E]—dc21 00-23520

ISBN 0-8050-6242-4
First Edition—2001
The artist used acrylics on illustration board to create the illustrations for this book.
Manufactured in China
10 9 8 7 6 5 4 3

To my dear "birthday club" friends:
Audrey, Lila, Marion, and Niki

—E. S.

To my aunt, Hioka Rumiko, with thanks

—H. T.

For my birthday, Aunt Betty gave me a new yellow shirt. "A yellow shirt!" squawked my best friend, Sam. "That's no fun!"

But Sam is wrong.

In my new yellow shirt . . .

I am a duck quacking, splashing through a big puddle of sun.

In my new yellow shirt . . .

I am a lion
stalking Mrs. Miller's garden,
scaring the crows with my ROAR!

Watch out!
Now I'm a taxi–HONK! HONK!–
zooming down the street.

When I'm tired of running and roaring, I become a lazy caterpillar taking a nap under a peach tree.

In my new yellow shirt . . .

I'm a daffodil
dancing dizzily
in the wind.

Or a fancy tropical fish
swimming round and round
in Sam's backyard pool.

In my new yellow shirt
I am a tennis ball
bounce-bounce-bouncing
at the playground.

Here comes the parade!
Now I'm a brass trumpet—
TOOT! TOOT!

In my new yellow shirt
I am a canary singing tweetily.

Then a butterfly fluttering away.
"You can't catch me, Sam!"

Shhhh!

I'm a golden treasure hidden in the dark, dark attic. Pirate Sam is searching for me.

Shhhh!

In my new yellow shirt . . .

I'm a silly banana
thumping about the house
telling jokes to my daddy.

And a yellow submarine
snorkeling up out of the bathtub.

At night in my new yellow shirt I join the fireflies.
I wink here, I wink there. I wink past
Sam's window.

At bedtime Mommy says,
"Time to take off
that new yellow shirt."
She lays it across the chair,
kisses me good night,
and tiptoes out.

But I'm not afraid.

My new yellow shirt is a smile of moon
in my very own room as I fall off to sleep.
"Good night, Sam."